Off to Oregon!

Penn Mullin

High Noon Books
Novato, California

Cover Design and Interior Illustrations: Michael Cincotta

International Standard Book Number: 1-57128-114-2

10 09 08 07 06 05 04 03 02
2 1 0 9 8 7 6 5

A number of High Noon Books, like this *Trailblazers Series*, are particularly appropriate as ancillary social studies materials. This may explain why the *Postcards Series* and the *Four Corners Series* are so very popular. Write for our free High Noon Books catalog that describes these and many other titles.

Contents

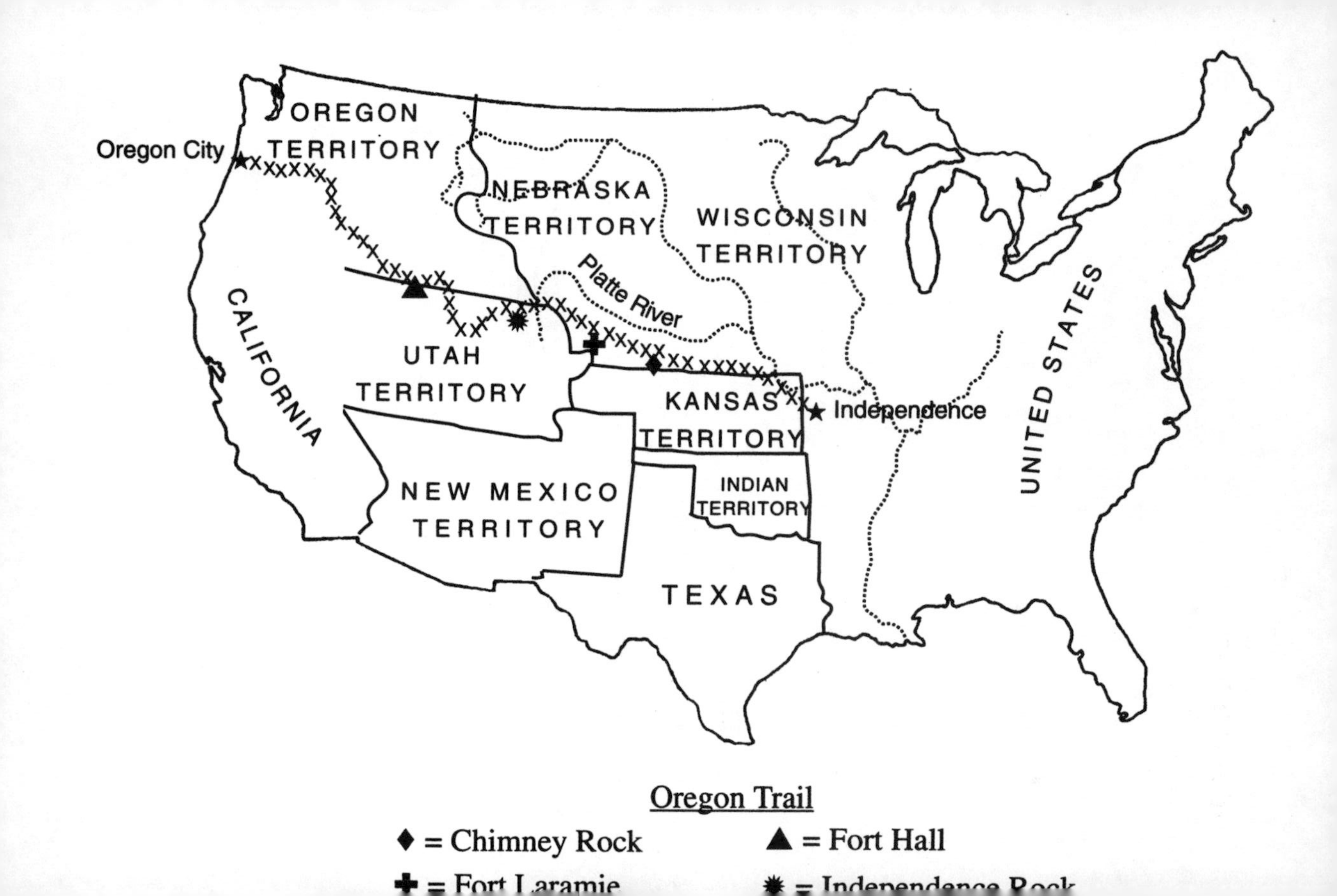
OREGON TERRITORY
Oregon City
NEBRASKA TERRITORY
WISCONSIN TERRITORY
Platte River
CALIFORNIA
UTAH TERRITORY
KANSAS TERRITORY
Independence
UNITED STATES
NEW MEXICO TERRITORY
INDIAN TERRITORY
TEXAS
Oregon Trail
♦ = Chimney Rock
▲ = Fort Hall
✚ = Fort Laramie
✹ = Independence Rock

CHAPTER 1

A Fresh Start

"Ben how would you like to go west to Oregon?" Pa asked.

Ben stared at his father. "Go to Oregon? You mean leave our home and leave the store?" Pa owned a big store here in busy Independence, Missouri. It was where the trail to Oregon began in 1851. People came down the Missouri River and got off here. Then they bought supplies and wagons for the long trip. Pa and Ben were busy opening their store for the day.

"Each day I sell flour and beans to men going to Oregon. I hear them say how rich the land is there. They say you can get 640 acres *free*!"

"What about Ma and little Ann?" Ben asked. "Does Ma want to go?"

"Yes and no," Pa said. "She will miss her friends and Gram and Gramps. But she wants to have our own farm. A wagon train leaves next week. They have room for us."

"But that's so soon! Can we get ready by then?" Ben asked.

"We have to. Time is short. It takes five months to get to Oregon. This is May. We must be off the trail before the snow comes," Pa said. "I've heard awful tales of people trapped all winter."

"Do we have a wagon yet?" asked Ben.

"I will buy one today and oxen to pull it. We must sell this store to get money for the trip. Two men want to buy it," Pa told Ben. "We are lucky. It will cost a lot of money to get the food we need." He took out a long list.

Ben read over his shoulder. "Seventy-five pounds of bacon for each of us? Two hundred pounds of flour! Do we really need that much?"

"Five months is a long time," Pa said. "Oregon is two thousand miles away. You'll work hard and get hungry. The food will go fast. Well, I'm off to see about our wagon now. Oh, I thought you'd like to know this. The Wood family is going to Oregon, too. So you'll have Tom with you to enjoy all the new sights."

"Tom is coming! Good!" Ben watched Pa leave the store. Now he was alone. He felt strange. My whole life just changed, he thought. I'm going to Oregon. It's all decided. I might never come back here. I might never see Gram and Gramps again.

What about the *Indians*? I've heard that some of them are friendly. But some are not. They are afraid of losing their lands. Sometimes they attack wagon trains. What if Ma or little Ann were to get captured? Maybe Pa will let me have a rifle! I'll be twelve soon. Tom and I could help guard the wagon train. Now Oregon was looking better! Ben couldn't wait to see Tom.

CHAPTER 2

Wagons Roll!

Dust was all over. It was in your mouth, hair, eyes. People yelled. Dogs barked. Cows bellowed. Whips cracked. The wagon train was about to leave.

Ben stood by his family's big wagon. He held tight to his dog. And he held the reins for Pa's horse. Pa was up in the driver's seat with Ma and Ann. The team of six new oxen were "yoked up" to the wagon. Five milk cows were tied behind. They would walk to Oregon. They would give fresh milk and butter along the trail.

Ben looked for the Wood's wagon. He and Tom planned to meet at lunch time. It felt good to have Tom on the trip. They were going to fish and hunt. But they had to get rifles first. Soon Ben would ask Pa.

A man called Frank Wade was captain of the wagon train. The people had chosen him that day. He was a tall, strong man. But he did not seem friendly.

A scout named Jed would help the captain. He wore buckskin clothes and rode a fast horse. Scouts knew how to get along with Indians. This was why wagon trains hired them. Ben wondered when they would see their first Indians.

Suddenly there was a loud gunshot. It was time to go! People cheered. Pa cracked his whip. The wagons began to roll. They were off to Oregon! Ben felt his heart pound. He looked up at Ma. She had tears in her eyes as she held tight to Ann. Last night they had said good-bye to Gram and Gramps. Maybe forever. It was a hard time. But this morning was better. Ma was smiling now. She waved at Ben as he walked beside the wagon. Ann held her old cat in her lap.

The wagons rolled in a long line of twenty-five. Ben's family was tenth in line. Each day they got a new number. In this way people took turns being in back with the dust.

Ben felt proud of their wagon. How did they

The wagons rolled in a long line of twenty-five.

get it all packed in just one week? There was not a bit of room left inside. Huge sacks of rice, beans, sugar, flour, and bacon were piled up. And Ma's spinning wheel and trunks, too. Her best dishes were packed in big barrels.

The wagon was covered on top with strong white canvas. The wagon "box" was made of wood. There were four large wooden wheels, too. A toolbox hung on the side. A feedbag for the cows was on back.

It's like a little house, Ben thought. All the things we need are right here. Tonight we'll camp out. This is going to be fun! Maybe Tom can share my tent!

The wagons rolled along the trail through

green fields and woods. The sun was warm. People were glad to begin the trip.

"Nooner!" the cry soon went up. The wagons stopped. People got out boxes of food. They sat down in a grassy meadow.

"I'm sure hungry!" Pa said. He put on some coffee to boil. "Good fire, Ben!"

Ben smiled. He knew the fire would be one of his big jobs on the trip.

"Ginger snaps!" cried Ann. She reached for a red tin box.

"Not until you eat your beans and beef," Ma said. "Just like at home."

Ben took a slice of bread. "Will you still bake out here?" he asked Ma.

"Of course! I'll bake in a big pot over the fire," she told him.

"Bread in a *pot*?" Ben asked.

"Yes! You'll love it!" Ma said.

"And roast rabbit, too," said Pa. "We'll have to shoot a lot of our meat."

Maybe this is a good time to ask about the rifle, Ben thought.

"Can I help hunt, Pa?" he asked. "I'm going to be twelve soon."

"We'll see. You might be good with a rifle. And I might need your help. We don't know what's ahead," Pa said.

"You mean *Indians*?" asked Ann.

"No, no, Ann. Now don't you worry." Pa got

up and poured his coffee. Then he walked down to the stream.

Well, he didn't say no about the rifle, Ben thought. But he is worried about Indians. I can sure see that.

"Chain up!" The captain yelled. Break was over. Frank wanted to make fifteen miles a day. "No rest days," he said. Ben knew Frank would be a tough leader. He would push them hard.

CHAPTER 3

Pawnees!

The prairie! They were on it now. It was like an endless wide green sea of long grass. It moved like waves in the wind.

"Look at that!" Pa said. "Now we're really in the West. It sure is pretty land."

Ben felt great. The trail had changed. This land was not like home at all. There were no trees anywhere. He was driving the team with Ma. Pa was riding beside the wagon.

Ma took off her big sunbonnet. "I want to

see it all. This old hat lets me just look straight ahead!" she laughed.

It felt good to see Ma laugh. Ben knew she missed home. But she was happy today. This was all new land. It was a new world.

All of a sudden Tom rode up. "Indians!" He pointed ahead. They could see four men on horses by the trail. The wagons stopped. Frank and the scout, Jed, rode up to the men. They all got off their horses. The Indians and wagon men handed things back and forth.

"They're Pawnees. They have come to trade," Pa said. "I hear they're friendly. Ma, get out one of your mirrors. They like them."

Soon the Pawnees were right up close. They

looked strong, with bare chests and deerskin pants. Their long hair was tied behind their backs.

Pa got off his horse and put out his hand. The Pawnees all shook it and smiled. Then they pointed to Pa's red shirt. They held out a thick robe made of buffalo fur.

"Pa, they want your shirt!" Ma said. "Give it to them. I'll make you a new one. That robe looks so warm!"

Pa took off his shirt and gave it to the Pawnees. They were so happy. Each one wanted to wear it. They gave Pa the robe and Ma and Ann some blue beads.

"I'll give them the mirror," Ma said. She held it up, and the Pawnees let out a yell. All their hands reached up for it.

Then the Pawnees gave Ben and Tom two bear claws on strings.

"Look at the size of this claw!" Tom said. "Must be from a grizzly bear!"

The boys put on their gifts and shook hands with the Pawnees. Ben looked down at the bear claw he wore. He did not want to forget this day. Now he did not feel afraid of the Indians. He saw that they were people just like him. For the first time he thought, this is *their* land. How do they feel that we are on it?

CHAPTER 4

The Crossing

It was hot. The sun blazed down. Ben walked in back of the wagon with his dog. His feet hurt. His new boots were almost worn out. He pushed the cows along with a stick. They were tired and thirsty. There had been no rain in a long time. They *had* to reach the Platte River soon. It was all people talked about. Pa worried about the oxen. What if they couldn't go on? There had been no rest days. Frank kept pushing the wagons hard.

Then Ben heard "Platte's ahead! The Platte!"

People passed the word. There were lots of cheers on the trail. Here was water! To cross the Platte was a big step on the trip to Oregon. They would follow it for almost 300 miles.

All of a sudden a wagon broke out of line! The oxen ran for the river. They were crazed for water. The driver could not hold the team. Then Ben saw it was Tom's pa! His wagon was going too fast. It would tip over. Where was Tom?

"Go help Ma hold our team!" Pa yelled. He raced his horse up the trail.

Ben jumped up on the wagon. Ma held tight to the reins. But the oxen pulled hard. They wanted to run. Ann clung to Ma and cried. Ben put his hands over Ma's and helped her pull. His hands burned. More teams went wild. Wagons tipped over. The sound of screams and oxen bawling was awful. Did Pa catch Tom's wagon?

Then they saw the river. It was so wide! There were islands all across it. Wagons sat stuck in the water. Loose cows and oxen stood in the mud. They bawled in fear. Ben and Ma were losing their team.

Some men raced up to the front of the team. They grabbed hold and slowed the wagon down. The team stopped. Ben ran for water for the oxen.

There was trouble at the river! Tom was screaming for help. He was out in the river on his horse. The water was deep. Ben knew Tom could not swim. All of a sudden there was Pa, swimming to Tom! He grabbed Tom off the horse. The horse sank from sight. Pa swam to shore. Tom hung on to his back.

Ben ran to get blankets. He wrapped them around Pa and Tom. People said, "It was quicksand! The horse ran off with Tom and got stuck in it." Ben felt a chill go down his spine. What if Pa had stepped into quicksand instead of swimming?

They still had the wide Platte to cross. Frank called a meeting. He said the river had deep holes and quicksand. And the current could be strong. He would show them the best place to cross.

The Wood's wagon had lost a wheel. Ben and Pa helped them fix it. They chained their two wagons to each other. Pa and Mr. Wood rode beside the wagons while their sons drove.

"Take it slow, now," Pa told Ben. "Let the oxen feel their way. We don't want them to step in a hole."

Ben was scared as they rolled into the river. He had heard of wagons that tipped over. People said the Platte was "a mile wide and an inch deep." But he knew that was not true. He had seen Tom's horse go down.

Ma and Ann sat with him in the driver's seat. Pa made sure the milk cows came on behind. The long line of wagons stretched out across the Platte. Once or twice a wheel would get stuck. Then the wagon would drop out of line. It was a

The water just hit the middle of the wheels.
Then it got higher.

slow crossing. Ben kept his eyes on the Wood's wagon in front. The water just hit the middle of the wheels. Then it got higher. Ben felt his heart pound. Why did Frank lead them this way? Would they be swept away? The water rose near the top of the wheels!

"I'm scared, Ma!" cried Ann. She looked down at the muddy brown water.

And then the water went down. The wagon rode high again. A cheer went up! Ben smiled at Ann. "See – we're just fine," he told her. "We're almost across now."

Frank called for a short rest and food on the shore ahead. Then they would join the trail again. They had miles to go before night came.

CHAPTER 5

A Close Call

"I can't find any wood, Ben," said Ann. "How can we make a fire tonight?"

"We'll have to use other things," Ben told her. He picked up some dried buffalo dung. "This burns OK. We may have to use it. There are no trees out here."

"Ick! I don't want to cook with that," Ann said. "I just won't eat tonight!"

All of a sudden they heard a sound like thunder. Then they saw a huge cloud of dust.

Dogs began to bark. Then they heard a gunshot. They knew that was the sign for danger. Ben and Ann ran for the wagon.

Frank and Jed yelled orders. "Buffalo stampede! Stay in your wagons. Stay in the circle. Hope that they turn!"

The cloud of dust came closer with a roar. Now Ben could see the big black shaggy buffalo heads. He knew a herd could plow right through a wagon train. Nothing would stop them. On and on they came. Thousands. The ground shook.

The air was thick with dust. You could not see. You just heard the roar coming at you. Ben sat frozen with fear. Ann screamed. Then the herd turned. It missed the wagons by feet. You could smell the buffalo. They were that close!

People cheered and cried as the herd roared on by. It ran for a full hour!

"How many were there, Pa?" asked Ann. "A million?"

"Seemed like it!" He laughed and wiped the dust from his eyes. "Well, it's way past supper time. I'll go milk the cows. You and Ben get your fire made."

"We left the buffalo chips out on the prairie," Ben said. "Let's go, Ann."

"Oh, no!" she groaned to her brother.

CHAPTER 6

Push on Ahead!

The trail was steeper now. There were rocks and deep ruts in it. The oxen had to work hard. People walked to make the load lighter. Only the drivers rode.

They still followed the Platte. It was a big day when they first saw Chimney Rock! It looked like a tall dark red tower. They could see it for many days before they got there. Ben and Tom climbed up on it to carve their names. This was a famous place on the trail. It felt good to make it this far. Oregon seemed closer now!

"Look at those hills ahead," Pa said one day. "Our oxen can't pull this load up them! We must lighten up. I hate to leave things behind. But we have to save our team."

Ma turned her face away. Ben knew this was hard on her. Her best things from home were in the wagon. And some must go. "All right, Pa," she said. She tried to smile. "We should leave the big trunks. Ann, help me take out a dress for each of us. They are for Oregon."

Other wagons did this, too. Piles of trunks and food were left. Treasures from home were left, too. There were many tears.

Ben helped Pa throw down bags of flour and

rice. They would just have to eat less. Ma's spinning wheel took up a lot of room. Ben hoped she could still keep it.

"Roll em!" came the cry. Frank was ready to go. There were big hills ahead. Ben, Ma, and Ann walked behind their wagon. Ma looked back once at her trunks. Parts of many lives now sat alone on the dusty trail.

The trail grew steep. The sun burned down. Their mouths were dry, filled with dust. The wagon went slower and slower. Could it make this hill? Would they have to take out more things? Then the wagon stopped.

Frank rode up. "Lighten your load. You can't hold us up." He rode on. Pa got off the wagon.

"OK. What shall we leave now?" he said. His eyes were sad. "I think the barrel of china has to go. I'm sorry. But it's so heavy. Ben, give me a hand up here." Ben climbed up. He and Pa rolled the barrel out. Three more food sacks had to go, too.

Ma was in tears. "I wish we had stayed home. Why did we ever leave?"

Pa put his arms around her. Ben felt scared when he saw Ma cry. Maybe they *should* have stayed home. Pa ran to start the team. They had to go on. Would the wagon move now? Ben heard the oxen groan and pull. The wheels creaked and slowly moved. Ma took Ann's hand and began to walk. She did not look back.

It was a long climb up the hill. There was no time to rest at the top. The train had to make Independence Rock by July 4th. If it didn't, it would not reach Oregon before the snow.

Day stretched after day. They walked behind the wagon. Hot long hill after hill. Ma and Ann had grown very thin. Pa always looked tired. Frank pushed the train hard. July 4th would be here soon.

But Fort Laramie came first. It was all people talked of. When will we get to the fort? Mail from home might be there! And there will be candy! A piece of pretty cloth. A new wheel. Coffee.

At last they saw the fort! It was a low wood

building two stories high. It had wide gates in front. Lots of Indian tepees sat around it. The wagons stopped and people went into the fort. Ma and Ann wore their best dresses. Ben was glad to see Ma look so happy.

The fort was a busy place. Many fur trappers and scouts were there. They told Pa that the Cheyennes on the trail were friendly.

"We have a letter from Gram!" Ma tore it open. It said, *Let us know when you get settled. We want to come out, too. We miss you so.* "Oh, Pa, do you think they could make this trip?"

"We still have a lot of trail ahead," Pa said. "It is hard to say right now." Ben knew Gram and Gramps could not make this trip. Ma most likely knew this, too. But no one said so right now.

They camped by the fort that night. The Cheyennes came to trade their buffalo meat with them. "It tastes good," Ben said. "But you have to chew it forever!"

They were off at dawn the next day. Now the talk was of Independence Rock. They were in the Wyoming lands. The plains stretched far and bare.

Ben still had no rifle. But Pa took him out to hunt. Ben learned to shoot well. He brought in sage hens and deer. When would he get his own rifle?

At last they reached it – Independence Rock! It was like a huge whale's back of red and white rock. But it was 10 times as big as any whale. There were cheers and gunshots. They had made it! Around the rock was a sea of white tops! Many more wagon trains were here.

"Let's go climb it!" cried Tom. He and Ben raced to the top. The wide smooth rock was covered with names and dates.

"Where shall we put our names?" Ben asked. "There's no room!" They stood on top of the rock and looked out at the plains. Ben felt proud. He felt good that they had come this far. He looked far into the west. It seemed to stretch forever. Was Oregon really out there? They carved their names and the date, July 4, 1851, on the rock.

Then they rushed back down the rock. Tonight would be like a big party. There would be lots to eat and fiddle music. Folks would shoot

"Let's go climb it," cried Tom.

off guns.

Ma was making a stew of dried beef from home. Ann was helping make a pie. Ben ran off to look for firewood. The oxen were unyoked. Then Pa got out his fiddle to tune it. There was a happy feeling in the air. Folks from other trains came to talk. Campfires lit the night sky. Now there was the sound of singing. Ben looked back at the wagons and smiled. Tonight he would watch Ma and Pa dance again. He might even ask Ann for a dance!

CHAPTER 7

Graves on the Trail

"Now we're on the west side of America!" Pa pointed to the broad grass plains ahead. "The water on this side of the South Pass flows to the Pacific Ocean. Behind us it flows to the Atlantic."

Ma said, "Let's all take a drink of that water! It's on its way to Oregon!" They all sat down by the creek and drank. Then it was back to the trail.

The next big stop was Fort Hall. There they said good-bye to friends who turned south on the California trail. They were off to look for gold!

Now the trail went along the Snake River. It would lead them close to Oregon! Ben didn't like the looks of this river, though. It was wide and fast.

They had seen graves all along the trail. It was always sad. A new baby died. A child fell from a wagon. But now they saw many graves. "Cholera!" People passed the word. Ben felt a chill go down his spine. He had heard of this killer. It could strike you in the morning. You could be gone by night.

"People wash clothes and water animals in the creeks. Then they drink the water. Cholera hits," Pa said. "We must boil all our water now."

And cholera came. There was no treatment, no cure. Wagons pulled off the trail and you knew. You wanted to stop and help. But Frank told you to keep on. There were many new graves now. People that you knew.

Then Pa woke up with an awful stomach pain. Ma's face went white with fear. "Ben, boil some water. We have to keep water in Pa. It's his only chance."

Friends came. But they could do nothing. Frank gave the signal. The wagons had to go on. "We'll catch up with you," Ben told them. Will Pa be with us? And what if Ma got sick? Ben was scared. He kept the fire hot and boiled water. Ann brought him wood.

Now they were all alone. The wagons had gone on. Pa was in awful pain. Ma kept cool cloths on his head. She made him drink all the time. The day wore on. Pa was out of his head now. He said strange things. Night was coming on. This was when people died. Ben kept saying, "Don't die, Pa. Don't die. You have to go on to Oregon. You have to."

And then Pa was quiet. He did not shake any more. And he opened his eyes. "Water, please," he said. He tried to sit up. But he was too weak. He smiled.

"Pa!" cried Ma. "You're going to live! Yes, yes!" Ben and Ann hugged Pa hard. They had been lucky – this time.

Pa was too weak to move. They stayed there for three days. Each day he grew stronger. One night he called Ben to him. "Son, go look under the wagon seat."

Ben's heart pounded. He reached under the seat and felt the rifle there. "Pa!" he yelled. "Is this for me?"

Pa smiled. "You have shown us you're a man. A man needs a gun. And we want rabbit stew tonight. So get hunting!"

CHAPTER 8

Oregon

They said good-bye to the Snake River at Farewell Bend. They had seen its falls and canyons. And crossed in its deep, fast current. Then they had caught up with the wagon train at Fort Boise (BOY-zee). Their friends were glad to see them. Pa drove the wagon and left the hunting to Ben. The family feasted on deer and elk.

One August day they stopped on top of a hill. A wide green valley and deep woods lay below them. Frank passed the word among the wagons. "*Oregon*! That's *Oregon*!" They were here! Ben let out a cheer. He looked at Ma. Her eyes were shining. Pa pulled Ann up into his lap. He pointed to the mountains ahead.

"Your new home is on the other side of those! They're called the Blues. We'll be over them soon!" he said. "Ma, you can get your best dress out!"

Ma smiled and got up beside Pa. She looked out over the rich green land.

"Pa, may I take the horse and ride down the hill?" Ben asked.

"Sure, son. Go on. And take your dog, too. We'll catch up to you!"

Ben raced over to Tom's wagon. The two

boys rode down into the valley. Ben felt the warm wind rush at his face. Oregon! They were here! It was all so new. And he was part of it.

They stopped and looked back up the hill. The wagons were spread out all along it. Ben felt proud of them all. He felt proud of himself, too. They had stayed with the trail. He knew they were not done yet. There were still the Blues to cross. But he knew nothing could stop them now. This was Oregon!